T0149331

Camp Sweet Tea

Adventures of Christina and Friends

Christina J. Moses

authorHOUSE®

AuthorHouse™
1663 Liberty Drive
Bloomington, IN 47403
www.authorhouse.com
Phone: 1 (800) 839-8640

Published by AuthorHouse   03/18/2016

ISBN: 978-1-5049-8381-5 (sc)
ISBN: 978-1-5049-8380-8 (e)

Library of Congress Control Number: 2016903720

Print information available on the last page.

Any people depicted in stock imagery provided by Thinkstock are models, and such images are being used for illustrative purposes only. Certain stock imagery © Thinkstock.

This book is printed on acid-free paper.

Contents

Acknowledgements

I first want to thank God for blessing me with the skills and ability to write. It is with great appreciation that I thank my entire family for their encouragement and support.

A huge thank you to my mother, Temeka Morrow, and my little sister, Sanoja Moses for always being my audience and number one fans.

I want to thank my kindergarten teachers, Mrs. Green and Mrs. Hinson for recognizing, encouraging and supporting my writing talents at a very early age.

I also want to give special thanks to my Aunt Melba and Uncle Steve, for making this project possible.

I really hope my readers enjoy this story as much as I have enjoyed writing it.

Christina J. Moses

Chapter One

The Day Before

Hi, my name is Christina. Guess what? I get to go to camp! It's going to be my first year. I'm a little nervous, but that will not get in my way of having fun.

The camp is called Camp Sweet Tea. I wonder why they call it Sweet Tea.

Anyway, my friends and I are so good to Miss Maria, our fifth grade teacher, she let us out of school for four weeks.

So… I am staying at camp for three weeks.

Okay, let's get to the story.

It was a beautiful day in Hickory Springs.

The birds were chirping and the crickets stopped bugging us.

I was at my new office club, called the Goddess Girls.

I'm the leader, or let's say, the president. Carrie was the assistant – or shall I say – the vice-president. Mabel was the secretary and the treasurer. Sometimes Rachel - who we call Ray - is president when I am out...which is rare.

I walked to the front, grinned and told everyone about camp.

"Camp? Um… I…," stammered Mabel. "I can't go I have to get a manicure at Sally's tomorrow and the next day I have to pack and…"

"Jeez Mabel slow the heck down! Where are you going?" Rachel asked.

"Miami…for four days to Aunt Maryanna's wedding.

"She ALWAYS wants EVERYONE to go to her weddings, she's been married 10 times," Mabel explained.

"Oh, goody! Tell your Aunt Maryanna good luck with this one!" I shouted.

I quickly mumbled, "Ok club meeting is over!" I was anxious to get home and prepare for camp.

Christina J. Moses

When I finished thanking Carrie for using her house club office I walked home to the great smell of my favorite... Spaghetti!! I ended up gobbling down my food... it was worth it!

The doorbell rang. OMG Sparky is here!!!

In case you haven't noticed, I'm an animal sitter; but I only sit dogs and cats. I don't play with snakes, snails or spiders. They don't pay me enough!!!

"Hey Sparky!" I said.

Sparky barked and Mrs. Neveragain gave me instructions before leaving her precious pooch with me.

When two hours were done Sparky left with Mrs. Neveragain… finally… I was getting tired of her.

Chapter Two

Camp Sweet Tea - Here I Come

The next day I woke up and got dressed and brushed my teeth. It didn't take long to do my hair. I put it up in a bun. Before you knew it, the bus came.

"See y'all in 3 weeks!!" I yelled to my mother and my little sister.

I ran out the house, stepped on the bus and sat alone – cause I wanted to.

Don't judge me! But why would you?

Before you knew it the bus stopped and a nice lady named Lucy Hammond asked us to get off the bus. The camp site was like soooo great it was very nice I had to admit I was impressed. But before I could see anything else, a tall lady named Donna told us to follow her.

She said, "If I give you a big fat sticker you're in my group."

She gave a bunch of us stickers and said, "C'mon friends, let's go to our Special Edition Cabins, and by the way - you guys are the lucky ones."

Donna had long smiles. We followed her to our "Special Edition Cabins" but when I looked in there was NOTHING special about these cabins.

I couldn't believe Donna lied. I REALLY wanted to say WHAT THE CRAP??????

I could have smacked her…. but I'm not violent.

Chapter Three

Roommates

Donna clapped her hands - we glanced at her and kept on talking.

Donna clapped harder, I guess that's how she's supposed to get our attention. But it sure wasn't working.

Donna clapped really hard. We finally gave her our full attention.

"We are going to introduce ourselves!" Donna loudly cheeses.
Everyone shrugged.

Carrie started first, "Hey everyone I'm Carrie Peach." She
waved like a beauty queen and did her little dance.

Everyone got to say their name.

"Sorry Campers we have to put Stephanie Summers in this group," Donna told everyone.

"Christina!!!!" Stephanie hollered like she hadn't seen me in ages. She gave me a big fat hug.

"O.K pick your bunk mate," Donna added, "And by the way, we are going to sleep in bunks – not beds."

Oh how formal.

Since I wanted to make new friends I picked Phoebe Carson, someone I didn't know.

"Would you like to be my uh ….. bunk mate?" I asked.

"Sure a great way for us to be friends," Phoebe said dryly.

She looked like she was bored.

I'm starting not to like her already.

Chapter Four

Camp Activities

Donna clapped, "Girls today it's time for us to make shirts, follow me!"

We all followed her into a big room outside.

A very cheery lady named Zoey screamed, "WE ARE GOING TO MAKE SHIRTS!!"

Everyone just sat down at tables and stared down at the t-shirts.

"Y'ALL CAN EVEN MAKE TWO!" Zoey yelled.

She really needs to stop.

Mallory almost fell out her chair as I grabbed my supplies and started doing my shirts. First I made one that said - *One of Selena Quintanilla's Biggest Fans!*

"Who's Selena Quintanilla?" asked Phoebe.

"The greatest singer in the whole world," I told her and my
other shirt said *SWAGGY GIRL.*'

'Seriously?" said Phoebe.

"Don't be jelly," I replied.

She is SO not my type of friend.

Three hours later another new girl joined our group - but she was snobby - only cared for herself. Her name was Mirabelle Melanie.

"Donna! I DON'T wanna go to this stupid camp, Mirabelle yelled, "and what happened to the so-called Special Edition Cabins?"

Donna frowned for the very first time, "your bunk mate is Stephanie Summers, if you're wondering."

Stephanie looked up from what she was doing, "WHAT?"

Mirabelle rolled her eyes. "That Stephanie has some UGLY clothes, that is so last season!"

Stephanie sighed.

I could tell that she wanted to call Mirabelle the "B" word.

Donna clapped her hands. "Campers, today we are going to see if we can go swimming."

She looked out the window. The sun was shining brightly and it was 98 degrees. "It's getting hot up in here." Donna murmured.

Everyone went into the dressing rooms to change into their swim suits. In a blink of an eye, we were running to the pool. Everyone jumped in, but I didn't. Even the Friendship Friends - or whatever they were called - joined in.

I sat on the edge of the pool. China walked towards me, "Hey Christina"

"Hey." I waved.

"So….." China started, "You gonna jump?"

I looked at my painted red nails, "Does it look like I'm gonna jump?"

China smiled like a Cheshire cat and stood up "Christina, can you please stand up!"

I glanced over at her and stood. Then China now behind me, pushed me in the pool.

I gasped!!!

"You're welcome!" China shouted.

I scowled at her. Mirabelle came out the pool giggling. I threw a rock at that brat. It hit her smack in the head.

Who's laughing now?

Actually who's laughing is Rachel, who's not even in my group. I guess she knew Mirabelle was the mean type. Anyway at least Donna didn't see me throw the rock - but Mirabelle told on me!

What a snitch!!!

We finally got out the pool, and I couldn't play on my tablet the rest of the day. I should have seen that coming. But I should've explained to Donna why I actually threw the rock - but I forgot - boohoo!

Chapter Five

Cafeteria Chatter

The next day was boring. Donna explained to us that we could only stay at Camp Sweet Tea for a week.

"Awww…" everyone but Mirabelle groaned.

"Well at least I get my nails painted at Molly Dolly's," Mirabelle said.

"You need to shut up," Kira whispered.

She was tired of the constant bragging.

Donna clapped her hands "Time for lunch, come on troopers!"

"Troopers, we aren't in the army," Mallory added.

We headed toward the cafeteria.

It was HUGE!!!

The tables and chairs were GOLD - yeah actual GOLD. I couldn't believe it! This is what I call GREATNESS!!! I, of course, got my favorite - peaches in a cup and some other stuff. I sat with Phoebe, Rachel and Stephanie. Well at least Mirabelle didn't sit with us.

"GUESS WHAT?! THERE'S A PEACH EATING CONTEST - JOIN NOW!!" Zoey screamed.

"Hey Christina, why don't you join," said Phoebe.

I grinned, "well I do LOVE peaches in a cup,"

"Well join!" shouted Rachel, "I'm sure you'll win"

"I don't want to guys, anyways have y'all heard of that new book called Madeline Polly, The life of a Princess by Roxy Foxx?" I said – changing the stupid subject.

Before you knew it, it was time to go.

"Come on girls," Donna said.

We all followed behind – just like her little ducklings.

Chapter Six

Ice Skating Drama

"Girls," Donna started, "We're going on a field trip – ICE SKATING!!"

Donna led us to a big yellow school bus.

"Hello everyone," the bus driver greeted.

We all spoke and jumped on the bus. It took ten minutes to get to the skating rink. The rink was cool – with colorful lights and a disco ball in the middle.

A woman named Georgia started smiling at us and said, "Hello everyone, I'm going to teach you how to ice skate."

She then clapped her hands and this big dog – a yellow golden retriever ran to Georgia with skates tied on his back.

Georgia says, "Thanks GiGi".

"Oh My Gosh, a dog with skates on his back…..how…how," yelled Donna.

 GiGi is a genius," proclaimed Georgia.

Then GiGi shocked all of us, when she said, "YUP I'M A GENIUS."

We all fainted in shock after hearing GiGi talk. Gigi woke us up by licking our faces.

"Eeeewwwww there's dog slim all over my face!" yelled Mirabelle.

In disgust, I said, "Why doesn't she just shut up!" As she wiped dog saliva from her face.

Georgia - still laughing – says, "So y'all want to ice skate or not?"

"WE DO," we all yelled together.

As Georgia gave us our skates, things didn't quite go as planned. We were slipping, sliding and falling like CRAAAZZZYYY. Taylor even broke her arm, Phoebe broke her ankle, Mirabelle broke both her legs, and I even twisted my ankle.

"Girls, girls are y'all alright?" Donna finally asked. "All of y'all HAVE to go!!!"

We all groaned.

Donna, Georgia, and some guys carried us to the bus and back to the camp.

Chapter Seven

Farewell Sweet Tea

"I'M NEVER GOING BACK TO THIS CRAP CAMP I'M SUEING" Mirabelle screamed.

Before you knew it, they called our parents to come pick us up.

Finally we were home and recovering from our stay in the hospital.

You're probably wondering why the camp is called "Sweet Tea.

Well, it's because sweet tea was the only thing the campers had to drink – not even bottled water. And you couldn't escape the tragedy of drinking sweet tea. It was tragic! Because it was the only drink and it was NEVER sweet enough. Yuck!!!

We all healed from our injuries and vowed never to go back to Camp Sweet Tea.

.